Benjamin T. Tanner

The Color of Solomon-What?

Benjamin T. Tanner

The Color of Solomon-What?

ISBN/EAN: 9783337319328

Printed in Europe, USA, Canada, Australia, Japan

Cover: Foto ©Andreas Hilbeck / pixelio.de

More available books at **www.hansebooks.com**

It is impossible to look at the above portrait and not be reminded of a remark attributed to the late Frederick Douglass. Gazing at a picture similar to the above, he said: "Well, if the Egyptians were not Negroes, and looked like that, they would have no trouble in passing for such in America."

Queen RAMAKA HATSHEPSU, NEMT AMEN was the daughter of Thothmes I, and of his half sister Aames. She would seem to have given early evidence of her capacity to reign, for her father, Thotmes I., early associated her with himself in the exercise of the sovereignty. Judging from her monuments she was of the XVIIIth Dynasty B. C. 1500, one of the greatest and most powerful of all the Egyptian dynasties.

THE COLOR OF SOLOMON—WHAT?

"My Beloved is White and Ruddy."

A Monograph.

BY

BISHOP BENJAMIN TUCKER TANNER. D.D.

INTRODUCTION BY

William S. Scarborough, LL.D.

PHILADELPHIA, PENN.
1895.

—o—

A. M. E. BOOK CONCERN,
631 PINE ST., PHILA.

DEDICATION

TO THE RISING SCHOLARS
OF THE COLORED RACE,
THE WRITER DEDICATES THIS MONOGRAPH
WITH THE HOPE
THAT THE SUBJECT WHICH IT DISCUSSES,
AND OTHERS AKIN TO IT,
WILL RECEIVE SUCH TREATMENT AT THEIR HANDS
AS WILL VINDICATE
THE COLORED RACES OF THE EARTH
AND SAVE THEM FROM THE DELUSION:
'THE LEADING RACE IN ALL HISTORY HAS BEEN THE WHITE
RACE."

"The times want scholars—scholars who shall shape
The doubtful destinies of dubious years,
And land the ark that bears our (people's) good
Safe on some peaceful Ararat at last."
—*Josiah G. Holland.*

INTRODUCTION.

It is one of the irrefutable proofs of the Negro's progress as well as of his ability that he is beginning to investigate and make researches for himself in all lines of literary activity. The day of helpless dependence is no more. A new era has dawned and the colored man has begun to add his own stint of original thought to the forces that determine the character and status of a people. He is rapidly changing his base and is no longer wholly relying upon the testimony of others as the reason for the faith that is in him, but is himself thinking for himself. This is certainly a most hopeful sign.

We need not multiply examples; for the author of this little treatise is ample proof. The Rt. Rev. Benjamin Tucker Tanner, D.D., is not only one of the foremost theologians of our times, but is indeed one of the best specimens of ripe scholarship the race has yet produced. His long years of experience as an editor, his wide, critical and thorough researches in historical, ecclesiastical, and linguistic lines, make what he has to say on any subject of more than ordinary importance. Thoughtful, discriminating and accurate, he writes not simply to carry conviction but to establish the truth with such force that conviction will be the inevitable result. The discussions that make up the following pages must therefore be of interest to all concerned and especially to the seeker after truth.

There are many theories as to the authorship of the Canticles (Song of Solomon), their object and character, and for this reason the subject is all the more difficult to handle. It suffices to say that from all the evidence that we have —external and internal—Solomon was doubtless of both Semitic and Hamitic extraction. Commentators, annotators, lexicographers, and textual critics, for the most part, avoid all references even though warranted by translation that suggest the idea of such extraction. This is one of the weaknesses of so-called modern interpretation—evasion or neglect— when the race question is introduced. It makes research fit the mold of preconceived notions. So much the more joyfully we hail one who seriously sets himself to the task of giving us the impartial discussion warranted by both the original text and context.

The subjects covered by the study of philology and ethnology, archaeology and paleontology, paleography and paleology lead out into fields that are as debatable as they are interesting. There is so much that is conjectural and so much that remains unsettled that philologists and scientists have been unable to find common ground and have, therefore, like the "son of Atreus, king of men, and the god-like Achilles, stood apart wrangling" among themselves. Philology, like ethnology may be considered as still in a transitional state. Neither has reached the dignity of a fixed science and cannot, as long as the origin and development of language and the history and relation of races remain shrouded in such mist.

Modern philologists are no more agreed than those of old as to the origin of speech if we are to judge from the amount of discussion pro and con. Plato and Aristotle, the teacher and the pupil, held opposite views. Plato, the idealist, reasoned as to what language ought to be; Aristotle the realist, discussed it as he found it. The same old story of the

vi

$\phi\acute{v}\sigma\epsilon\iota$, ("by nature") and the $\theta\acute{\epsilon}\sigma\epsilon\iota$ ("by assignment," or "agreement") one or both—which? Aristotle declared that language was the result of an agreement. In themselves, words were meaningless and their significance depended upon what men by common consent decided they should mean.

The late Professor Whitney of Yale in his masterly reply to Max Muller on the Science of Language and in an able paper printed in the Transactions of the American Philological Association discusses at some length the $\phi\acute{v}\sigma\epsilon\iota$ and $\theta\acute{\epsilon}\sigma\epsilon\iota$ theory. He held that words in their individuality exist $\theta\acute{\epsilon}\sigma\epsilon\iota$, and only $\theta\acute{\epsilon}\sigma\epsilon\iota$: but the $\theta\acute{\epsilon}\sigma\iota\varsigma$ itself is $\phi\acute{v}\sigma\epsilon\iota$ if we may include in $\phi\acute{v}\sigma\iota\varsigma$ not only man's natural gifts, but also his natural circumstances. In this sense only, and with these limitations, it is proper to answer $\phi\acute{v}\sigma\epsilon\iota$ to the question as to the existence of speech. We might add argument to argument to show the speculative character not only of philological science but ethnolgical as well.

With the Bible as a starting point and with the light thrown upon the subject by philological and ethnological research we may regard it as pretty well settled that the numerous tribes and classes of men, throughout the earth formed but one species; that they have all come from a single pair—Adam and Eve—and that the differences constituting the variety of race may all be accounted for by natural causes—all of which, to one desirous of information, cannot be otherwise than conclusive.

The Pre-Adamite theory is not only *wholly* untenable but unscriptural. It has nothing to recommend it. It is simply an easy attempt to settle a momentous question. The Jebusites, the Amorites, the Girgashites, the Hittites, the Hivites, the Perizzites, were not at all, *per se*, averse to intermarrying with the Israelites. There was no personal prejudice so far as the people themselves were concerned for they frequently intermingled. Solomon was the son of Bathsheba, formerly the wife of Uriah the Hittite, while he himself married an Egyptian princess. a daughter of Pharaoh. In fact both social relations and political relations grew exceedingly close at times throughout Biblical history, and from this and similar practices in ages following it may be reasonably inferred that neither Solomon nor his Egyptian bride possessed unalloyed racial characteristics.

We are told that nearly every complexion is still found in Egypt—"the yellowish Copt, supposed to represent the ancient Egyptian, the swarthy villager, the dark wild Arab, the dead, dusky soft black of the Nubian, the coarser, more jetty black of the Negro and still further, the weather-blacked, spirited and often finely chiseled face of the southern Arab. The natives of Egypt are generally dark and far southward toward Ethiopia, almost black ; yet those of high rank, being protected from the sun are pretty fair, and would be reckoned such even in Britain ;" at least so says Matthew Henry.

We can heartily bespeak for this little volume a cordial reception, feeling sure that its perusal will not only result in pleasure but in profit, arousing thoughtful minds to give more attention to a line of investigation that should occupy more and more the scholars of the Negro race.

W S. SCARBOROUGH,
"Tretton Place," Wilberforce, Ohio.

viii

PREFACE.

---◇---

BY THE AUTHOR.

It is just possible that among the thousands, nay millions for whom we stand in this discussion, only a small per cent. of them have ever heard of the *odium theologicum*. Unconsciously, however, they have all entered fully into its spirit the spirit of a positive odium that has been defined as "stronger than dislike, weaker than hatred, more active than disfavor, disgrace or dishonor, more silent than opprobrium and more general than enmity."

And wherefore this *odium theologicum* on the part of the Afro-Americans of the Republic? The reason is not far-fetched, but on the contrary, is directly at hand. These Afro-Americans, and singularly enough the Christian portion of them especially—by reason of its superior intelligence, entertain odium toward the theologians, for the reason that they put contempt on the word : "Whosoever, therefore, shall break one of the least of these commandments AND SHALL TEACH MEN SO, shall be called least in the kingdom of heaven" (Matt. 5: 19); and it is therefore at their door that they lay chiefly the burdens of woe they have been compelled to bear.

In the past these theologians not only condoned slavery, but made it, as it were, a divine institution, in that they argued that the curse pronounced upon Canaan, legitimately fell upon the Negro race of Africa and of the world. Even the just-minded Adam Clark is heard to ask, referring to the judgment pronounced upon the Gibeonites (Josh 9: 21): "Does not this refer to what was pronounced by Noah against Ham and his posterity? Did not the curse of Ham imply slavery and nothing else?" To the same import are the words of Newton in his dissertation, On the Prophecies. Having convinced himself that the curse was really pronounced on Ham,* the plain words of Scripture, however, to the contrary,

---

*My suspicion hath since been confirmed by the reverend and learned Mr. Green, Fellow of Clare Hall in Cambridge, who is admirably well skilled in the Hebrew language and Hebrew metre, and hath given abundant proof of his knowledge and judgment in these matters in his new translation and commentary on the Song of Deborah, the prayer of Habakkuk, etc. He asserts that according to Bishop Hare's metre, the words, *ham abi*, are necessary to fill up the verse. He proposes a further emendation of the text by the omission of one line, and the transposition of another, and would read the whole paragraph thus, according to the metre.

> 'And Noah said,
> Cursed be Ham the Father of Canaan ;
> A servant of servants shall he be to his brethren.
> And he said,
> Blessed be Jehovah, the God of Shem ;
> For he shall dwell in the tents of Shem.
> God shall enlarge Japheth ;
> And Canaan shall be his servant."
> —*Newton On the Prophecies, p. 18.*

In the presence of such intellectual surgery of the word of God as is here hinted at, who can wonder at the infidelity of the last century---who wonder that one of the unbelievers (Dr. Wells) was profane enough to say that to "obtain the prophetic spirit, they played upon music and drank wine"---and this in reference to the very prophecy under consideration.
—*Leland's Deistical Writers, p. 57.*

x

he says : "The whole continent of Africa was peopled princi-pally by the children of Ham ; and for how many ages have the better parts of that country lain under the dominion of the Romans, and then of the Saracens, and now of the Turks? In what wickedness, ignorance, barbarity, slavery. misery, live most of the inhabitants? And of the poor ne-groes, how many hundreds every year are sold and bought like beasts of the market, and are conveyed from one quarter of the world to do the work of beasts in another?"

The logical sequence of such statements as these, is to make the slavery of any or all the Hamitic races, as we have said, a divine institution, the very strength and boast of the ystem when it was in its glory.

Nor are the theologians of to-day doing a whit better than those of the past generation. As we have seen, those of the past not only assented to our bondage, but bolstered it up by their interpretation of Scripture.* These of to-day not only assent to and practice caste, but join hands with a "science so-called" that strives to put us outside the pale of Adamic and Noachic humanity, and declares in favor of our non-Hamitic descent—a science that incidentally puts it : "As

---

*The Christianity of this country as exhibited in the churches is not the Christianity of Christ. It is a man-degrading and Ne-gro-hating Christianity. In the South it lived and flourished side by side with slavery for two hundred years and never had any quarrel with it, and in its presence to-day the Negro is robbed, lynched and murdered without rebuke or remonstrance from these Christian pulpits.
—*Frederick Douglass in letter to Rev. J. W. Beckett, Oct. 28, 1891.*
Mr. Douglass broke with the American Church, and with Amer-ican Christian dogma when he saw it made to sanction and defend the enslavement and bondage of a brother, with its horrible con-sequences. It was then that he had advanced beyond his coun-try, and its church, to where Christ to him was larger than Creed, and his Christianity transcended his churchianity. And from this point Mr. Douglass never retrograded but he never ceased to reverence the God of humanity, as he saw God.
—*Rev. J. T. Jenifer, Douglass Funeral Address.*

neither type is represented with the characteristic color and features of the negro, we must regard both types as belonging to the Cushite or Hamitic race, akin to the Egyptian and probably of the same common origin."*

The editors of Teachers' Quarterly, Methodist Episcopal Church, proclaim that it is not yet certain "that the Negro descended from Ham."

The significant feature of this is, that this theory is given to the children of the Sunday schools, indicating the strong trend of the current of their wish, that the Afro-American and the Negro in general should be put beyond the pale of a common humanity : and that, too, despite the fact that a large per cent. of them have accepted civilization, and bear, not only the white man's name, but share, to no small extent, his blood.

" An Ammonite or a Moabite," commanded Moses to Israel by the authority of God, "shall not enter into the assembly of the Lord; even to the tenth generation * * * * because they hired against thee, Balaam the son of Beor from Pethor of Mesopotamia to curse thee. Nevertheless the Lord thy God would not hearken unto Balaam ; but the Lord thy God turned the curse into a blessing unto thee, because the Lord thy God loved thee (Deut. 23: 3–5)."

Nor will we, even of these theologians, quote what the following verse says: "Thou shalt not seek their peace nor their prosperity all thy days for ever."

Israel carried this out to the letter. Says Dr. William Smith :† " The hatred in which the Ammonites were held by Israel is stated to have arisen partly from their opposition, or rather their denial of assistance to the Israelites on their ap-

---

*Twelfth Memoir of Egyptian Exploration Fund, p. 24.
†O. T. Hist. p. 92.

proach to Canaan. But it evidently sprang mainly from their share in the affair of Balaam. But whatever its origin, it is certain that the animosity continued in force to the latest date."

But it shall not be so with us. The sunlight of love is too high and too widespread; and the God who came to our help and blew to the winds their interpretations in the past, the same God is on the throne to-day; and as it was with our fathers, so shall it be with us.

> "Daughter of Zion, the pow'r that hath saved thee
> Extolled with the harp and the timbrel should be,
> Shout, for the foe is destroyed that enslaved thee,
> Th' oppressor is vanquished and Zion is free."

The booklet we here present is but the beginning. Thousands of our young men, and young women, too, for all that, are in the great schools of this and other lands. We cannot doubt that not a few of them will take up this discussion where the men of this generation leave off, such men as Blyden and Perry, Crummell, and Scarborough, and carry it on to such success as will compel the world not only to be willing to retain us in the common brotherhood, but in a way to see with Swedenborg* who declares the African to be superior to the rest of the world in "interior judgment" —in a way, interpret to our benefit the words both of David and of David's Lord:

"The stone which the builders rejected is become the head of the corner." (Psl. 118: 22).

" And behold, there are last which shall be first, and there are first which shall be last." (Luke 13: 30).

---

*True Christian Religion: Swedenborg, p. 541.

SECTION I.

PRELIMINARY

In no country in Christendom, except the United States of America, would the color of a man be deemed a subject worthy of consideration. In all other lands it is race or nation; the moral or intellectual status that is discussed. They say with the poet:

> " But give us now and then a MAN,
> And we will crown him king,
> Just to scorn the consequence,
> And just to do the thing."

In the United States, however, that that is mightier than manhood—mightier than race or nation, morals or intellect, is the negative quality of the color of the skin. "Is he white?" is Ali Baba's "Open Sesame," to all circles, be they industrial or fraternal, social or religious.*

---

*Exceedingly *apropos* to what we have said is what the Philadelphia *Press*, in its issue of February 24, 1895, says in its reference to the death of Frederick Douglass. Its words are:

" The death of Frederick Douglass has been followed by wide public notice of the honors he had received, the consideration with which he has been treated and the positions he has filled.

But it is worth while remembering, in the interest of justice and equality, twin duties of the Republic, that these honors and this consideration were both infinitely less than he would have received in any other civilized country in the world, though more than one American goes through life imagining that "the

14

The condition of things arising from such a fact, is the one and only excuse to be advanced for discussing the otherwise senseless question of Solomon's color ; a king who reigned quite three thousand years ago. To give formal shape to this excuse, we say, we discuss the color of Solomon for three reasons :

The *first* is, that it is well enough to know the truth of a matter, even though it be trivial; and for the truth's sake.

The *second* is, in a land like ours, where anything like greatness is universally denied to all who are not of the white race; or, against all facts to the contrary, such characters and peoples as attain to incontestable

---

Republic is opportunity" for all its citizens in a better sense than in any other lands. As a matter of fact, it is not, where color is concerned.

In England, with his ability as a speaker, Frederick Douglass would unquestionably have become a member of Parliament, and he might easily have been knighted, as men darker than he have been. In France he would have found Dumas, a man darker than himself, honored through life in every social circle and after death one of the few whose statue stands in the Theatre Francais. If, as might easily have been the case, Douglass had been elected to the French Academy, he would have found there, now and in the past, men of his race. In no corner of France and in no part of Europe would he have found the hotel, the theatre, the railroad car, the school or the home in which he would not have been accepted on his merits as a man and his manners as a gentleman.

This simple equality and justice exists in all other civilized nations. When like even-handed justice is dealt here the Negro question will be solved, and no other solution can give peace because none other is just."

greatness are declared members of that race,* it is well enough to know if there be any exception to such a rule.

The *third reason* for our inquiry is, that our translation of the Book of books, both the Authorized and the Revised editions of it, makes Solomon to be white, when it is absolutely certain that according to the di-

---

*As proof of this statement, the case of the Egyptians is in point, who are now claimed by ethnologists as of the white race, notwithstanding the fact of their Hamitic origin, the color of their skin and their notably curled and crisped hair. Says Pierre Henri Larcher, in his Notes on Herodotus : "*The Egyptians have black skins and crisped hair.* This passage is so positive, that I cannot conceive why Mr. Browne should explain it by 'a tint somewhat deeper than that of the Greeks.' The epithet 'atrati,' given by Ammianus Marcellinus, favors my explanation rather than that of Mr. Browne ; but this epithet is not the only one ; I give the entire passage : ' *Homines autem Ægypti, plerique subfusci sunt et atrati.*' 'The greater part of the Egyptians are of a deep color bordering on black.' This writer speaks of the Egyptians of his own time. He lived about 800 years after Herodotus. Egypt, subject in the time of our historian to the Persians, became afterwards so to the Greeks and to the Romans. The mixture of these various nations had changed the natural color of the people. They were no longer black, but 'subfusci,' bordering on it. Mr. Browne endeavors to support his opinion by the color of the mummies ; but he should prove that the mummies were of an age anterior to Herodotus, or at least prior to the time when this mixture of the Egyptians with their conquerors had effected their complexion. The portion of a mummy, preserved in the cabinet of St. Genevieve, authorizes me to suggest this question. It consists of the foot, the leg and half the thigh of an infant two or three years old ; the surface is quite black, and so smooth that it may be compared to a fine Chinese varnish. This mummy decides the question." * * * * * * "But what sets this question entirely at rest is, that the Colchi were black, and had woolly hair, as Herodotus tells us. St. Jerome and Sophronius, cited by Bochart, call Colchis the second Ethiopia ; and Sophron-

vision of the human family made in said Book, he did not belong to the White race, and all things being equal could not personally have been white, as that word is popularly understood. We refer to the translation of what is written in the Song of Songs (5: 10):

> " My beloved is white and ruddy,
> The chiefest among ten thousand.''

It is in place to say that this is the answer Solo-

---

ius, in his life of St. Andrew, informs us that towards the mouth of the Apsarus, and on the banks of the Phasis, there were Ethiopians; now, the Hebrews bore not the slightest resemblance to these people.

" Herodotus is not the only author who maintains this opinion. Pindar had before him named these people $K\varepsilon\lambda\alpha\iota\nu\omega\pi\varepsilon\iota\varsigma$ This is: 'with dark faces.' On which the Scholiast remarks, that being originally from Egypt, they were black, $\mu\varepsilon\lambda\alpha\nuo\chi\rhoo\varepsilon\varsigma$ ''

In addition to the above, Constantine Francois Volney says as much and more, claiming that the Egyptians were not only dark skinned or black, but were real Negroes. His words are, in reference to that celebrated passage of Herodotus: "that is, that the ancient Egyptians were really Negroes, of the same species with all the natives of Africa; and though, as might be expected, after mixing for so many ages with the Greeks and Romans, they have lost the intensity of their first colour, yet they still retain strong marks of their original conformation.'' * * * * Thus to the black race we are indebted for the arts, sciences, and even for speech.''

It was Arnold L. Heeren who maintained that the Sphinx is a representation of an Ethiopian, and it must be confessed that he who will look with his eyes and not with his prejudice, as Wendell Phillips was accustomed to say, will be constrained to agree with him.

—*Larcher's Notes on Herodotus, Euterpe II. § CIV Also Beloe's Herodotus.*

mon's "black but comely" bride, is supposed to have
made to those who asked:

> What is thy beloved more than another beloved,
>   O thou fairest among women?
> What is thy beloved more than another beloved,
>   That thou dost so adjure us?

The adjuration alluded to was:

> ' I adjure you, O daughters of
>   Jerusalem, if ye find my beloved,
> That ye tell him that I am sick of love."

To speak colloquially, the adjuration of the queen
would be after this manner:

> "I adjure you, O daughters of Jerusalem,
>   Because my beloved is a white man,"

a veritable morsel of sweetness to all the caste-loving
of the nation.   Was Solomon white? as is declared in
this translation of the original:

> " My beloved is white."

To him who questions the correctness of this translation, endorsed, though it be, by the learned Revisers
of Jerusalem Chamber, Westminster Abbey, come
helps or proofs not a few, and to them we beg to call
attention.

ETHNOLOGICAL HELPS OR PROOFS.

In the light of Ethnology, the translation: "My beloved is white and ruddy," if it be understood to refer to what we might call the primal color of the king, can scarcely be correct; and for the reason that Solomon did not belong to the White race, as this race is Biblically, and we might say, scientifically defined, and popularly understood; and this being so, as we have already said, Solomon could not be personally white.

Upon the question of the divisions of the common race of mankind, there are differences not a few. According to Karl von Linne there are four divisions or races of men and founded upon the color of their skin: (1) European or white; (2) American or copperish; (3) Asiatic or tawny; (4) African or black. George Louis Leclerc Count de Buffon increased the divisions by one, having five, *to wit.* (1) The Hyperborean (the inhabitants of the Polar region, Eastern and Western Asia, etc.); (2) Southern Asiatic; (3) European; (4) Ethiopian; (5) American. Johann Frederick Blumenbach also numbered the races at five: (1) Caucasian; (2) Mongolian; (3) Ethiopian; (4) American; (5) Malay Baron Cuvier (Georges Chietien Leopold Dagobert) will have but three races. (1) Caucasian; (2) Mongol; (3) Negro; and those of Renè Primevere Lesson and Robert Gordon Latham are the same. Julien Joseph Virey has two; Bory de Saint Vincent has fifteen; Dr. James Cowels Richard has seven. The last to be mentioned is Dr. Daniel G Brinton, who regards*· "the following as the most appropriate scheme in the present condition of science for the sub-division of the species Man in its several races or varieties. I. The Eurafrican Race. *Traits.*—Color white, hair wavy, etc. II. The Austafrican Race. *Traits*—Color black, hair woolly, etc. III. The Asian Race. *Traits*—Color yellowish or brownish, etc. IV The American Race. *Traits*—Color coppery, hair straight, etc. V Insular or Litoral Peoples. *Traits*—Color dark, hair lank, etc.

It is impossible to scan this long list—and quite as many more could be added, and not call to mind what Paul says (1 Tim. 6: 20): "O Timothy, guard that which is committed unto thee, turning away from the profane babblings and oppositions of the knowledge (science) which is falsely so called." Are we asked: What does this knowledge or science teach

---

*"Races and Peoples." p. 97.

as to the divisions of the human race? Our answer is: The same as the Bible would teach of the days of creation, if some of its writers said it occupied three days, others four days, others five days, others ten days and still others fifteen days: The same as the Bible would of the origin of the race, if some of its writers said, all sprang from one pair; others, from two pair; and yet others from three pair. And lastly, the same as the Bible would teach of the universality of the flood, if some said it covered all the mountains under the whole heaven; others, that this range or continent was excepted; and still others another range or another continent. Manifestly all would agree, that in such case, the Bible could not be relied upon in its teachings. And how conclude otherwise in regard to science? Are not the differences and contradictions which we have imagined of the Bible, veritable realities of science? And yet, their name is legion, who lift up their voice in favor of science and against the Bible; when the teaching of science in regard to the division of the race is absolutely *nil.* If such differences and contradictions were found in the Bible, how readily would this same legion, cry out against it. But the many writers of the Bible are a unit upon this question, as they are

upon every other; and that, too, despite the fact they
were not all of one nationality, to say nothing of one
civilization. They lived in different ages; spoke different languages; and were under conditions as varied
as we can well imagine human life to be. Not so, the
men of science. These have all lived within one and
the same century, are men of the same race and largely
of the same nationality; and, as to their condition, it
is as nearly one and the same, as can be. Yet they
are as far apart in regard to a question they have un-
dertaken to decide, as are the poles: only approaching unanimity as they approach the division incidently
made and sanctioned by the Bible; *to wit.* the three-
fold division. But let us return from this brief ex-
cursus.

The antediluvian world was incapable of division;
being purely Adamic. Not so, however the post-
diluvian world which was Noachic, through Shem
and Ham and Japheth, the respective fathers of the
races whose ultimate homes were the three conti
nents, Asia, Africa and Europe. It is not, of course,
to be denied that there was mixing not a little among
the descendants of these patriarchs before they finally
took possession of their allotted homes. We all
know that Hamitic races figured largely in the rehabil-
itation of Southern Asia; and that Japhetic races did

the same among the nations of Northern Asia and those
bordering on the Mediterranean, in what is known as
Asia Minor, especially. Ultimately, however and long
before the Hebrew monarchy took its rise, each race
took possession of the continent God designed, as both
the Old and New Testament Scriptures assert; the Old
* * * "of these were the nations divided in the earth"
(Gen. 10: 32): The New * * * * "and he made of
one every nation of men for to dwell on all the face of
the earth, having determined their appointed seasons,
and the bounds of their habitation" (Acts 17: 26).*

---

*"Two facts are prominent in the outline of the population of
the world, which are given in Genesis x: the tripartite divisions
of the nations into the descendants of Japheth, Shem and Ham;
and the original centre of all these races in the mountains of
Armenia, where Noah came forth from the ark. That the rec-
ord is meant to include all the peoples of the known world, is
clear from the concluding words: These in their *nations* and by
these were the nations divided in the earth after the flood."
* * * * * * *
The territories of JAPHETH lie chiefly on the coast of the
Mediterranean, in Europe and Asia Minor, " the isles of the
Gentiles;" but they also reach across Armenia and along the
Northeastern edge of the Tigris and Euphrates valley, over Media
and Persia. The race spread Westward and Northward over
Europe, and at the other end as far as India, embracing the
great Indo-European family of languages.
The race of SHEM occupied the southwest corner of Asia, in-
cluding the peninsular of Arabia. Of his five sons, Arphaxad
is the progenitor, both of the Hebrews and of the Arabs and
other kindred tribes, whose origin is recorded in the book of
Genesis. North of them were the children of Aram (which signifies *high*) in the highlands of Syria and Mesopotamia. *Ashur*
evidently represents Assyria ; and the Eastern and Western ex-
tremities' were occupied by the well-known nations of the
Emæansly (children of *Elam*) on the southeastern margin of

It is substantially this tripartite division of the race, that Linnæus and Cuvier and Lesson and Latham accept; and not because it is Biblical, but because it is in keeping with what their eyes behold and true science endorses. According to this division, therefore, Solomon belonged not to the white or Japhetic race, nor to the black or Hamitic race, but to the yellow or Shemitic—not to Europe nor to Africa, but to Asia; and so he could not have been a white man, especially in the American signification of that phrase.

Upon this question of the color of men, as science presents it, let us dwell for a moment—the color especially of the peoples known to have inhabited the Solomonic land and continent. It is in place, however, to say that we are indebted to the Japhetic or

---

the valley of the Tigris, and the Lydians (children of *Lud*) in Asia Minor.

The race of Ham (the *swarthy* according to the most probable etymology) presents very difficult but interesting problems. Their chief seat was in Africa, but they are also found mingled with the Semitic races on the shores of Arabia, and on the Tigris and Euphrates, while on the north they extended into Palestine (the land of the Philistines), Asia Minor and the larger islands, as Crete and Cyprus. In Africa *Mizraim* is most certainly identified with Egypt; Cush with Ethiopia above Egypt; and *Phut* probably with the inland peoples to the West. Among the sons of Mizraim, the *Lubim* correspond to Libya; and those of Cush represent tribes which crossed the Red Sea and spread along the southern and eastern shores of Arabia, up the Persian Gulf and the Valley of the Tigris and Euphrates.

—*Smith's O. T. Hist. pp. 56-59.*

white race for all our facts; for it is they alone in this day who do all the delving, all the discovering, all the translating, and all the concluding; and we all know that in all things that pertain to the race with which they are identified, they proceed on the thought that "blood is thicker than water," with them "all roads lead to Rome."

> "If horses and oxen had hands and could
>   work in men's fashion
> Then would horses depict gods like
>   horses and oxen like oxen."*

And yet the information this master race of the hour gives, is all we have or will have until some Negro Scarborough push himself into the dead past and see its truths and facts with his own eyes and give to the race and the world his own conclusions.

But what say these Japhetic savants in regard to the color of the peoples of the past? We begin with Prof. A. H. Sayce.† "Closely connected with the color of the hair and eyes, is the color of the skin. This is the most obvious of all the distinctions between race and race, and was naturally the first to attract notice. The oldest attempt to construct what we may call an ethnographic chart—that in the tomb of the Theban prince Rekbma-Ra about a century be

*"The Races of the Old Testament." p. 21.
†Xenophanes of Colophon. B. C. 540.

fore the birth of Moses—(and almost three centuries after the advent of Abram into Aram or Syria),—divides mankind into the black Negro,the *olive-colored Syrian*, red skinned Egyptian and the white Lybian." The word of Dr. E. B. Tylor is substantially the same :† "The color of the skin has always been held as specially distinctive. The colored race portraits of ancient Egypt remain to prove the permanence of complexion during a lapse of a hundred generations, distinguishing coarsely but clearly the types of the red brown Egyptian, the *yellow-brown Canaanite*, the comparatively fair Libyan and the Negro." Lieut. Gen. R. Strachey, F. R. S., says,* in referring to the peoples of Asia: "Next in numerical importance to the Mongolians are the races which have been called by Professor Huxley *Melanochroic* and *Xanthochroic*. The former includes the dark-haired people of Southern Europe and extends over North Africa, Asia Minor, *Syria* to Southwestern Asia and through Arabia and Persia to India. * ∗ * * The Melanochroi are not considered by Professor Huxley to be one of the primitive modifications of mankind, but rather to be the result of the admixture of the Xanthochroi (who

---

†Art. "Anthropology." Brit. Ency. Vol. II. p. 111.
*Art. "Asia." B. E. p. 696. ₰ 113.

have fair skin, blue eyes and light hair) with the *Australoid* whose hair is dark, generally soft, never woolly * * eyes and skin are dark, the beard often well developed, the nose broad and flat, the lips coarse and jaws heavy ''

According to science, then, the people of the land of Solomon, the Syria of Greek literature, the Aram of Hebrew, were "olive colored," if we are to believe Professor Sayce; or "yellow brown," if we are to credit Dr. Tylor; and if we allow Professor Huxley to diagnose their case, sprang from the fair skinned Xanthochroi on the one side and the dark, coarse-lipped, heavy-jawed Australoids on the other. In so far as it is possible to conclude, the color here assigned must be the color of the progenitors of Solomon; for what saith the "law and the testimony" in regard to those from whom he was descended?

We are not to be supposed unmindful of the fact that these scientists will not have the Syrians of whom they speak to be one and the same with the Hebrews. This may be true. But we are not discussing any religious, political, or national distinction. On the contrary we are discussing, purely and simply, the color of a people of one of the continents, and physically of one and the same race, even the Shemitic; of whom

Brinton writes: "The Asian Race. *Traits*—color yellowish or brownish etc."*

And yet we are most free to say: First, that in so far as history teaches, such peoples as white Syrians and colored Syrians, distinguished as such, are utterly unknown. And second, appealing as we have said to the "law and to the testimony," as will be seen below, we are perfectly sure of our Aramæans or Syrians of the Hebrew type; nor can the force of this be broken, save by an appeal to some pet theory or special pleading.

"And Isaac was forty years old when he took Rebekah, the daughter of Bethuel the Syrian of Paddanaram, the sister of Laban the Syrian, to be his wife (Gen. 25: 20).

And again:

* * "And Isaac sent away Jacob: and he went to Paddan aram unto Laban, son of Bethuel the Syrian" * * (Gen. 28: 5).

And lastly, Moses would have Israel as a nation say when they had attained the Promised Land:

"And thou shalt answer and say before the Lord thy God, A Syrian ready to perish was my father, and he went down into Egypt and sojourned there,

*"Races and Peoples." p. 98.

few in numbers; and he became there a nation, great, mighty and populous" * * (Deut. 26: 5).

And quite a thousand years after this, do not we hear Herodotus speak of the Hebrews as Syrians, in the matter of circumcision: "The Phœnicians, and Syrians of Palestine, acknowledged that they borrowed the rites of circumcision from the Egyptians" (Euterpe, CIV).

With such facts as these before us, it is not necessary that we greatly concern ourselves with the criticism that would so extend the Aram of the Bible eastward as to exclude the Syria of the Greeks—not necessary after the real scholars of the world have spoken and made the two lands Aram and Syria one and the same as may be seen below:—

"Aram or Aramæa seems to have corresponded generally to the Syria and Mesopotamia of the Greeks and Romans. * * * * A native of Aram was called *Arammi*, an Aramæan, used of a Syrian and of a Mesopotamian."

—McClintock and Strong. Art. *Aram*.

"Aramæa* * * embraced the countries known to the Greeks by the various names of Syria, Babylonia and Mesopotamia."

—The International. Art. *Aramæa*.

"Aram, such as it occurs in the Old Testament, comprises all those peoples which inhabited Syria and Mesopotamia, north to the Taurus, east to the Tigris; but as these peoples never formed a political unit, the name is not used collectively, but only with reference to some particular tribe or region or state."

—Schaff–Herzog Ency Art. *Aram*.

The testimony, however, of Gesenius, especially as it is endorsed by Tregelles, is the most conclusive of all, as touching our view of the case. Defining the word *Aram*, these lexicographers agree in saying: "This ancient and domestic name of Syria, was not altogether unknown to the Greeks. See Hom. Il. II. 783, Hesiod. Theog 304; Strabo XIII, 4, § 6; XVI, 4, § 27   The name of Aramæa however extends more widely than Syria, and also includes Mesopotamia, although Pliny (V 15, § 12), and Mela (I, 11), give the same more extended limit to Syria. When it simply stands Aram, we should generally understand western Syria, or that properly so called."

In perfect agreement with this, is what that other great lexicographer, Buxtorf, briefly says in his " Lexicon Hebraicum et Chaldaicum."   "*Aram*, the proper name of a man, Gen. 10: 22 , thence the coun- try was called Aramæa, Syria."   And it is a little singular and altogether worthy of mention that Aram was among the lineal ancestors of this same Solomon.

The Hebrew people descending from Shem, are therefore of Asia, of Syria or Aram, which fact excludes the idea that they were either white or black, but yellow or olive. This being true of the people generally, it is necessarily true of Solomon particularly; for *ab omne disce* is quite as true as is *ab uno disce*.

And yet, it is just possible that a word quite as effective in settling what we have in hand as any already said, may still be uttered. Would you believe it that the probabilities are that Solomon was not of pure Shemitic blood, but of blood Shemo–Hamitic? She who had been the wife of Uriah the Hittite, Bathsheba, was his mother. The Hittites came of Heth, the second son of Canaan, the fourth son of Ham; and of them Deane† says: "In figure they are short and thick-set, of a yellowish complexion, with black hair, but without beards. Such in appearance were Abram's friends, the children of Heth at Kirjath-Arba." Was Bathsheba a Hittite? In the list of those Hittites individually mentioned in the Bible—the list as given by Dr. Strong, her name does not occur. But there need be no surprise at this, when the seeming

---

†Abram: His Life and Times. Rev. Wm. J. Deane, M. A. p. 35.

care to discount Hamitic blood is remembered. That the question of her race is still an open one, may be seen by the facts in the case. Her grandfather was Ahithophel the Gilonite. It is in vain that we seek to know the race or nation of this man; only we know him to have been one of the trusted counsellors of David. From this, however, it is not to be inferred that he must be a Hebrew, for David respected talent; and in the management of his kingdom, it is said that even the blood of his and his father's old foes, the Canaanites was no bar to advancement either in his court or in his army,* as instanced in the case of Abimelech and Uriah.

Of Ahithophel, however, one who has given the matter much study† says: "In regard to his family relationship, it is almost beyond doubt that he was the grandfather of Bathsheba, and it has been suggested as probable that he was first introduced at court through this connection"—the probability here alluded to, finds support in the fact that he is never mentioned in connection with the court until after Bathsheba's entrance; whereas, it is not at all likely that one so able, had he been a Hebrew, would have

---

*See McClintock and Strong, Vol. IV. p. 279.
†Art. Ahith. B. E. Vol. I. p, 422.

remained unknown. The words, also, of Batchelor
Blunt, Margaret Professor of Divinity, Cambridge,
throws a ray of light upon the probability of his Gen-
tile or Hamitic extraction. He says: * "Now from
2 Samuel eleventh chapter, I learn that Uriah the
Hittite had for his wife Bathsheba, the daughter of
one Eliam (the son of Ahithophel the Gilonite). I
look upon it, therefore, as almost to amount to a certainty that Uriah had married the granddaughter of
Ahithophel. I feel that I now have the key to the
conduct of this leading conspirator; the sage and
fondest friend of David, converted by some means or
other into his deadly foe—for I now perceive that
when David murdered Uriah, he murdered Ahithophel s grandson by marriage and when he corrupted
Bathsheba, he corrupted his granddaughter by blood."
Putting all these facts together they can scarcely be
accounted for other than by seeing in Ahithophel one
in whose veins the blood of Canaan flowed; and whose
love of clan was supreme; for who can imagine a Hebrew honored as was Ahithophel, taking sides not
only against his king the anointed of God, on account
of taking his granddaughter into his Harem—more of
an honor then as now in all oriental lands, and for

---

*Blunt's Coincidences. p. 144.

circumventing the death of Uriah of an uncircumcised
race. The probabilities are, therefore, in favor of the
thought that Ahithophel himself was of Hittite extraction, and blood to him was more than adoption.

The father of Bathsheba was Eliam. In the book
of First Chronicles (3: 5) it is given as Ammiel. And
here we think we find the first decisive proof of our
position, for Ammiel is as Dr. John McClintock says,
the name of "a non Israel person, while Uriah," he
adds significantly, "was a Hittite." One Hittite,
marrying the daughter of another Hittite!

We come now to Bathsheba. Of her, it is first to
be said, that she was the wife of a Hittite ; second-
ly, as we have seen she was the daughter of a man
bearing, if not a Hittite name, certainly the name of
a person of non-Israelite extraction; thirdly, she herself bore a Hittite or Canaanite name, Bathshua. "It
is perhaps worth notice," says authority,† "that
Shua was a Canaanite name (Com. 1 Chr. II: 3, and
Gen. 38: 2–12)." "We know but little of her," says
Canon Farrar,* "but that little is wholly to her dis-
advantage. If her name was originally Bathshua;
this may possibly imply that she was, in part at least,
of heathen extraction."

†McClintock and Strong, Ency. Art. Bath. Vol. I. p. 696.
*"Sol. His Life and Times." p. 7

So much for the blood maternal that was in him; but how about the blood paternal? The writers of the lineage of.David make a point as it were to tell us that he was the great grandson of Ruth the Moabitess, a people of blood the most mixed for the relation be· tween them and the Hamitic tribes by which they were surrounded, was the most cordial. How thoroughly alien she felt herself to be, may be judged from the "unconscious rhythm"* of her soul, when she sings :

" Insist not on me forsaking thee,
    To return from following thee
    For whither thou goest, I will go ;
    And wheresoever thou lodgest, I will lodge :
        Thy people is my people
        And thy God my God :
        Wheresoever thou diest, I will die.
        And there will I be buried.
So may Yahveh do to me,
            And still more,
    If aught but death part thee and me."

Ruth I : 15–17.

How thoroughly alien both in blood and religion the pious of Israel felt her to be, may be judged from what the Chaldee Targumist writes. Referring to the marriage of ·the sons of Elimelech, he says: "And they transgressed the edict of the word of the Lord, and took to themselves alien wives of the daughters of Moab." (See P C. Ruth Ch. I. V 4).

---

*(P. C. Int. Book of Ruth).

Lastly and yet most forcefully of all, how thoroughly
alien she was, may be seen from the divine provision:
" An Ammonite or a Moabite shall not enter the assembly of the Lord ; even to the tenth generation shall
none belonging to them enter into the assembly of the
Lord" (Deut. 23 : 3).*

And so it will be seen that on both sides, non-Jew-
ish blood flowed in the veins of Solomon; and all
non Jewish blood meant blood, the more "colored,"
and not as Prof. Sayce would have it, who concedes a
possible infusion of foreign blood, but would have
the infusion come from Japheth in that he gives him
red hair; and not from Ham nor Shem. But it is
yet to be shown that there were any Japhethites in all
that region, while it was a very Hamitic centre. From
the fact of David committing the care of his parents
to the king of Moab, we have really his assent to

*And yet, in the face of an ancestry with a percentage greater
or less of Hamitic blood, Prof. Sayce has the effrontary to say
and the London Religious Tract Society unconsciously to publish
the word "Races of the Old Testament" p. 74: "David we are told
was blonde and red-haired," and refers you to the reading
(Sam. 17: 42): "And when the Philistine looked about, and saw
David, he disdained him : for he was but a youth and ruddy, and
withal of a fair countenance." Three things we are here told of
David : The first, refers to his age—he was a youth: The second, refers to his color—he was ruddy—or reddish : The third,
to his appearance—he was of a fair countenance. The original
of the word, *fair*, here, is, yaphey, and means, beautiful, and
beautiful ONLY. See Strong's Concordance, Heb. and Chal. Dict.
Nos. 3302-3303.

what has been here said. "And David went thence to Mizpeh, of Moab: and he said unto the king of Moab, "Let my father and my mother, I pray thee, come forth, and be with you, till I know what God will do for me" (1 Sam. 22: 3).

Surveying this whole matter, we may be assured that by accepting the theory, if indeed we be forbid to proclaim it as a fact, of Canaanitish blood in the veins of Solomon, a reasonable solution will be found:

First: for the great favor with which the Hittite people were received at the court both of David and Solomon. Of this fact we have only to remember the names of Ahimelech and Uriah. Referring to this last, Dr. James Strong says: "He was doubtless a proselyte, and probably descended from several generations of proselytes; but the fact (of his position) shows that Canaanitish blood was in itself no bar to advancement in the court and army of David "*

Second: Solomon's passion for women, manifestly of darker hue than were the women of Israel of pure Israelitish blood. Chief among them being the daughter of Pharoah; concerning whom we find it convenient to say: *First*, she was black according to her own words; but not, indeed, as our white translators

*McC. & S. Vol. IV., p. 279.

of the Bible give them.   According to these, she is
made to say:

> "I am black but comely"

What she really says is:

> "I am black and comely
> O ye daughter of Jerusalem."

Second: She was black according to Herodotus who
writing of the Egyptians says: "The Egyptians   *   *
*   *   are black and have short hair and curling."[*]
He had previously said as much   "When the Dodo-
naei tell us that the dove was black; they give us to
understand that the woman was Egyptian."[†]

Quite as dark complexioned as was the daughter of
Pharaoh, was that other Hamitic princess with whom
he became enamored, even the Queen of Sheba; to
say nothing of the Canaanitish women, many of them
Hittites with whom he filled his Harem; and all of
whom were of swarthy color.

Third: If Solomon had no Hamitic blood in his
veins, how account for those plaits of hair:

> "Thy cheeks are comely with plaits of hair"—
> (S. of S. 1: 10.)

and especially how account for that "bushy" hair, to
say nothing of the deep gold color of his "head"—

*Herod. Euterpe CIV.
†Larchner's Notes, Euterpe. II. p. 331.

may not the face be said to be a part of the head
—alluded to in his famed epithalamium?

" His head is as the most fine gold
His locks are bushy and black as a raven."
(S. of S. 5: 11).

His bushy locks:⸱ The word here for ·bushy is
תלתל *taltal*, which signifies "a trailing bough (as
pendulous):—bushy;" or "the pendulous *branches of*
palms, with which flowing locks are compared" The
root of this word, *taltal*, is תלל, which signifies "to
pile up, *i. e., elevate;* or, "to heap up, to make high."
To interpret the description which Solomon himself
here gives of his hair, especially in the light of the
root word, it is impossible, not to conclude that the
bushy hair, (*piled up*, in ringlets, as it were) or curled
and crisped as commentators give it; points unerringly
to Hamitic or Canaanitish ancestry

Our concluding word, is: To insist that Solomon
was of the white race and personally a white man, is
not only to contradict all the facts given above, but
it is to contradict what he himself plainly has his
bride to say. She proclaimed him to be ruddy or
reddish, the color of all pure Asiatics, be they of the
occident or orient.

LINGUISTIC HELPS OR PROOFS.

———

A thousand years hence. or ten thousand if you please, no one need be in doubt as to the color of any notable individual of any class of persons, be he never so worthless. Nor is the reason far fetched. As intimated before, color is everything in America, at least in the United States portion of it. The first thing the American newspaper, the magazine or the book, presumes to tell of "John Smith," is that he was white or colored, as the case may be; that is, the failure to say he was colored, is accepted as saying he was white. Therefore in the future, however, far reaching, there will be no trouble in knowing the race or color of any one whose name shall have out lived the waste of centuries. Not so the past. The people of those days, were altogether too sensible to concern themselves about it; too just to discriminate against it, and altogether possessed of too lofty a sense of the

40

worth of merit as to allow them to bestow it for the possession of that that is purely negative. As the result of such a course, it is exceedingly difficult to know what was the real color of individuals and often of whole classes of persons.

> " For a' that, and a' that,
> It's coming yet, for a' that—
> When man to man the world o'er,
> Shall brothers be for a' that "
> —*Burns*

If, in those ancient times, notable men were wise or foolish, strong or weak—were successes or failures it would be known; but whether they personally were white or colored, or black, you are not told. We saw in Guild Hall, London, the bust of a pure Negro; but who was he? All inquiry at the hand of the guide was in vain It is more than probable that it was made to represent some great character in the Roman invasion of Great Britain; and it is quite possible that all students of history have read of him; yet the fact of his color was lost sight of by the pagan writers of Rome, in the presence of the greater fact that he was one of their successful leaders. We have just lost Frederick Douglass. But the fact of his connection with the colored race, is made prominent, although it is well known that everybody was already aware of it. The press, both secular and religious vied with each other in saying he was "colored," the "mulatto," etc So far were the pagan intellect and morals above such trivial facts, that it is to be questioned if any language of the past, has words expressive of the mingling of the common blood of the common race—no word expressive of Mulatto, of Quarteroon, or Quinteroon or Octoroon.* Such, are the inventions of these latter years; and they are exceedingly significant of the fact that in the administration of the Lord's grace to fallen man, which He has been pleased to place largely in the hands of the Japhetic races, they have been singularly unfortunate in their ability to eradicate race pride and have the world act upon the fact that in God's eyes there is neither Jew nor Greek, bond nor free—simply, man.

Nor were the ancient Hebrew peoples any exception to what was true of their pagan neighbors. They were tremendously racial in their affections—as we all know, and in so far as the nations of Canaan were concerned, were so by direct command of God and in the interest of religion. Speaking by the mouth of Moses,

*"The persons of African descent are further classified, according to the degrees of colored blood, as follows: blacks 6,337,980; mulattoes 956,989; quadroons 105,135, and octoroons 69,936."
—Compendium of Eleventh Census: 1890.

God said to them: (Ex.34: 11-16): "Observe thou that
which I command thee this day: behold, I drive out before thee the Amorite, and the Canaanite, and the Hittite, and the Perizzite, and the Hivite, and the Jebu-
site. Take heed to thyself, lest thou make a covenant
with the inhabitants of the land whither thou goest,
lest it be for a snare in the midst of thee: but ye shall
break down their altars, and dash in pieces their
pillars, and ye shall cut down their Asherim: for
thou shalt worship no other god: for the Lord, whose
name is Jealous, is a jealous God: lest thou make a covenant with the inhabitants of the land, and they go a
whoring after their gods, and do sacrifice unto their
gods, and one call thee and thou eat of his sacrifice;
and thou take of their daughters unto thy sons, and
their daughters go a whoring after their gods, and
make thy sons go a whoring after their gods "

But in all this, there was not the least speck of
what is known as color prejudice. The supposed "in-
stinctive repulsion" of these latter days had not
manifested itself. Nor was the outcry of Miriam and
Aaron against the marriage of Moses to the Ethiopean
woman any exception. On the contrary it may char-
itably be supposed that it was done in keeping with
their conviction as to what God had previously said

and which we have quoted above. But the Divine
displeasure made manifest the fact that God would
not have them interpret his law to the hurt of Moses
or in the interest of what might have been a caste
spirit.*

In keeping, therefore, with what we have said above,
the Hebrew language has no word comparable to mulatto, quadroon, quinteroon, etc. Commenting, as we

---

*"Besides vindicating Moses and rebuking his detractors, the
Lord put a mark of his displeasure on Miriam. The ringleader in
the sedition she bears the brunt of the punishment. She has af-
fected to abhor her sister-in-law as unclean; she is herself smitten
with leprosy, a disease loathsome in itself, and which entailed
ceremonial defilement in the highest degree. This done, the
cloud of the Divine presence rose as suddenly as it had come
down. Miriam and Aaron stood before the tabernacle utterly
confounded, till Aaron was fain to humble himself before his
brother, saying:—We have done foolishly, we have sinned; forgive
us, and do not let the sad affair go further; have pity on poor
Miriam especially, see how pitiable a sight she is. 'Like the dead
thing of which the flesh is half consumed when it cometh out of
its mother's womb.' Moses was not the man to resist so touching an appeal. Miriam was healed; but she was shut out from
the camp as an unclean person for the space of a week, as the law
prescribed. The lesson lies on the surface. Do not give harbour
to envy because of the welfare or honour of your neighbor, rather
'rejoice with them that do rejoice.' It is not always easy to rejoice when some one younger, or of humbler birth than ourselves
is exalted above us. Nor is the difficulty lessened when the person exalted is of our own kindred. Nevertheless envy must be
cast forth. The author of all gifts and honours is God. To envy
the receivers is to rebel against him and provoke his displeasure.
And God's ordinary method in punishing envious pride is to in-
flict some peculiarly ignominious stroke. When Miriam swells
with pride she is smitten with leprosy."
—*Rev. Prof. W. Binnie, D.D., P. C. Com. Numb. 12: 2–13.*

are, upon the word, "white," as it appears in the Canticles, we say:

In the Hebrew language there are but five words that can in any way be made to stand for the idea of "white," which word appears in our translation of the Old Testament, say forty one times. These words are: (1) לבן laban; (2) הרי choriy; (3) צחר tsachor; (4) דר dar and (5) ריר riyr.

Let us take these words up in the order in which they are here given: The first, as it is pronounced in English, is *laban*. Of the forty one times the word "white" appears in the Old Testament, it is the translation of this word in no less than thirty three times; making it next to possible for one to conclude that substantially the Hebrews had but one word to express the idea of white—white, pure and simple—and in all these thirty three times, it is never given as the color of a man save when it refers to the curse of leprosy: "and if the bright spot be WHITE in the skin of his flesh, and the appearance thereof be not deeper than the skin * * * * then the priest shall shut up him that hath the plague seven days" (Lev. 13: 4). Save where *laban* is used metaphorically and is intended to convey the idea of white or whiteness, such as the making of bricks from *white* and *chalky* clay (Gen.

11: 3), or referring to a kind of tree or shrub having white leaves or a whitish bark, thought by some to be the *white poplar* (Gen. 30: 37 Hos. 4: 13), or to *frankincense* from the whiteness of the purest of this article (see Lev 2: 1 etc. etc.), or the idea of pray·ing, *purging, cleansing* from the filthiness of sin (Dan. 11: 35. 12: 10), it is never translated other than *white*. What we mean to say and do say, is, that in the Hebrew mind, the idea of *white* is inseparable from this word.

The next word, pronounced, in its root word, *charar* is the only one next to *laban* that can in any way be said to mean, *white*. As the places where it is used are few, we can afford to refer to them. Once it is trans· lated, *pale* (Isa. 29: 22), once as *white bread* (Gen. 40: 16), once as *white cloth* (Esth. 1: 6), and once simply as *white*, referring to Mordacai's dress (Esth. 8: 15).

Tsaohar, as it is pronounced, is next. According to accepted authority, such as Gesenius, Tregelles, etc., the signification of the root word, tsachach, of this word is: (*1*) *To be bright, to be white.* (*2*) *To be sunny, to be shone on by sun.* The signification, of *shining* and *being bright* is the one signification of all that is extended into the various forms of the word;* that of *white*,

_____
*See Strong's Hebrew and Chaldee Dictionary Nos. 6795-6708.

being lost sight of. And yet in the Old Testament it is given as *white*, in three places: In the book of Judges (5: 10) we read * * * "ye that ride on white asses." The second instance is that of Canticles (5: 10) and now under consideration; and the third is the "white wool" of Ezekiel (27: 18). It is altogether worthy of note, that while such meaning as *dazzling, sunny, bright, glow, glare, parched*, are almost universally given in the Lexicon, yet when the translation is given, *white* is preferred, when it is only by inference that this word can be made to apply at all.

Dar comes next, and is translated, *white* in the book of Esther (1: 6), as descriptive of the pavement in the king's palace. It is generally thought to mean "a pearl, especially a large one from the root of the word which means *to shine*. Nor would pavements inlaid with pearls be foreign from Asiatic luxury "I prefer, however, to understand," says William Gesenius, "*a stoen* like a pearl."

Next and last, is the word, *riyr*, from the root word, *rueor* (roor), to *slaver* (with spittle). The sole signification of this word, is connected with the idea here given; with the solitary exception of Job (6: 6): "Is there any taste in the WHITE of an egg?" The marginal reading is, and it is doubtless the more correct: "Is there any taste in the juice of purslain?"—conveying as the last does, the idea of *running*, which is inseparable from the root signification of the original.

With the above facts before us, what the color which the writer of the Song of Songs, none other than Solomon himself, had in mind, we confess would be difficult to decide, had we no other way of reaching a conclusion than from the words themselves. And equally difficult would it be to decide which of these words, excepting the two last mentioned, we would use, if we wished to put the word, white, as we understand that word in relation to race into the mouth of his bride. Fortunately, however, for us and for the position which we take, we have two, if not three, additional ways of meeting both these difficulties and of concluding the matter aright. The first is that to which attention has already been called and treated under the head of ethnology. The argument of ethnology is, that however much poetic license may be allowed, yet must the poet in the main conform himself to the facts that are fundamental in the case. The fact, in this case to which conformity is due, is, that Solomon being a Shemite, an Asiatic, a Syrian in the language of the Bible itself, could not have been white, in the sense of being a member of the Japhetic or white race And to this fact, even poetry the form of language used in Canticles, must defer.

Our second method of meeting the difficulties in question is according to what is called *conceptualistic probability;* and it relates entirely as to which one of the words in question Solomon would have been most likely to use, supposing him to have wished to convey the idea that he was white, that is, a white man, according to the American usage of that term. According to the law referred to above, the law of probability, Solomon undoubtedly would have used the first of the words we have noted, *laban.* What says this law? "The greater the frequency with which a specific event occurs in the long run, the stronger is the expectation that it will occur in a particular case." Now let us apply this law to the question under consideration. The writers of the Old Testament, from first to last, extend over a period of considerably more than fifteen hundred years. They had, therefore, a "long run" in the reference, not only to white, but to other colors besides; and in the use of the words employed to designate them. "*Adam,*" signified "to be red," to Moses, and it was "to be red" to Zach·

4

ariah quite a thousand years after Moses. *"Tekeleth"* was "blue" to Moses and it was "blue" without a single exception to all who had occasion to refer to that color down to Ezekiel. Without pretending to say that the rule here suggested, held unbroken sway in regard to all the colors, it will be sufficient for our purpose to show that it uniformly held sway which undoubtedly is the case; especially so, with the word *laban*, signifying to be "white." As has already been shown, this was the one word of all given for the idea of white: and so generally was it employed, thirty-three out of forty one times, that its use was next to unanimous. According then to the law of probability, Solomon would have used this word, if he had wished to speak of that that was really white. Did he do it? The books of the Bible accredited to Solomon are: Proverbs, Ecclesiastes and Canticles or The Song. In them the word *white*, occurs but twice; first in Ecclesiastes (9 : 8):—"Let thy garments be always *white*; and let not thy head lack ointment;" and in the Canticles (5 : 10):

"My beloved is *white* and ruddy."

A reference to the original will show that this two-fold mention of white, though interpreted by one and the same word, is really not one and the same word in Hebrew   In Ecclesiastes, the word used is *laban*; in the Song, it is *Tsachach*. We have already alluded to these words and their use; but as their relation to the matter in hand is now acute, additional remarks are necessary   As to the first, in Ecclesiastes, it is quite sufficient to repeat what has alread been said, that *laban* is the one word in the Hebrew mind that stood for white, pure and simple. Would Moses (Exodus 16 : 31) describe the *whiteness* of manna, *laban* was the word he employed. Would David (Psl. 51 : 7) pray for unspotted cleanliness from sin; or God himself promise such unspotted cleanliness by the mouth of Isaiah (1: 18); or Joel (1: 7) refer to trees barked to barren whiteness, each employed the word in question. In fact there is but a single instance where the translation of this word varies from that of the word *white*, or what is akin to it; and then the word *fair*, is employed. Notably enough, that instance is found in the translation of what Solomon wrote—but the proof is self-evident, that he meant white, as any may see :

> "Who is she that looketh forth in the morning
> Fair as the moon."
>
> —*S. of S.* (6: 16).

It is reasonable to suppose, and withóut the least intent of putting words into the mouth of Solomon, that had he purposed stating the fact that he was personally white, and so belonged to the white race, he would have used this word, *laban*; as the great law of probability requires that he should. It is certainly far fetched to have him use a word of so wide a range of meaning, as *Tsachach*; and we say this with all deference to the splendid acquirements of Dr. James Strong, who in what he has shown, is himself the strongest witness against his own position, that *Tsachach* "plainly," means *white*. When David uses it (Psl. 68: 6) its meaning is given as "parched:"

"But the rebellious dwell in a parched land."

By Isaiah it is variously used:

" * * "their multitude are *parched* with thirst" (5: 13), also * * * "like *clear* heat in sunshine" (18: 4).

As used by Jeremiah it is * * * "a *hot* wind from the bare heights in the wilderness, etc.," (4: 11).

Other illustrations could be given, in which the most varied signification of this word would appear; the one tendency of which would be to show the utter improbability of Solomon using it, if he wished to proclaim himself white and of the white race. On the contrary, had he wished or intended so to say, there can scarcely be a doubt that he would have used *laban*, the word he employed in the book of Ecclesiastes when he wrote:

Let thy garments be always *white.*

In concluding the Helps or Proofs, which Linguistics offer, none can fail to observe that the weight of it is decidedly in opposition to the thought that Solomon intended to convey the idea we are combating, *to wit*, that he was a white man, as the average American reader of Canticles will conclude from reading the words which form the basis of our Monograph.

What is said of his hair, *bushy, curled, crisped,* especially our remarks upon it, would strictly come under this section. But so evenly and aptly does it fit in where we placed it,* that although it may seem somewhat out of place under Ethnology, yet do we prefer to allow it to remain there and invite the reader of this section to refer to it, as it is largely linguistic in its kind.

We conclude this section with the remark: To argue other than we have done, at least to reach any other conclusion than the one we have reached is to utterly disregard the plain statement of this Egyptian bride. She plainly declares her beloved to be ruddy or red. Now, the Hebrew word for which this stands,

*See page 39.

is the one that stands for this color in all the Old Testament Scriptures. It is, *Adam*, and referred primarily to the color of the earth from which Scripture teaches the first man was made. Nor did it ever loose this primary signification. Wherever the color, *red*, is in question, it is without an exception, the one word that is used; for what is said in Genesis 25: 30 and Psalm 75: 8 and Isaiah 27: 2, can scarce be claimed as exceptions. Indeed it can be stated that they are no exceptions at all.* And this is the word the bride employs. Why then should it be gainsaid? And yet to gain his point Japheth is given to this thing. At least, he stands charged with it and by one who knows. Says Gesenius of Halle, in defining this word: "Whiteness and ruddiness belong to the description of youthful beauty; hence it is a mistake to apply the word, *Adamu* in Lamentations 4: 7, as meaning clear whiteness as Bochart and Ludolf have done. But those who defended this opinion would hardly have adopted it, had they not been rather too desirous to attribute to *Pheninim*, the signification of pearls." The word then of the bride should be allowed to stand. Men should not be too desirous to prop up their theories at the expense of giving it a

---

*Strong's Exhaustive Concordance, Nos. 2447: 2560-61.

signification, that in all honesty, it has not. Like to the Hebrew nobles in the days of Jeremiah, he was

* * "more ruddy in body than rubies, its polishing was that of sapphire."

VERSIONAL HELPS OR PROOFS.

Are we interrogated as to the color Solomon really meant to describe? We confess it to be a difficult interrogation; and for two reasons. At best color is most difficult to describe, especially the color of flesh, for flesh is more subtle in tint and texture than wax (or other such objects), as a great art critic has said.* The cause of this difficulty is that colors are simply different shades between two extremes, white and black. "Pure white light and darkness," says Prof. Edward S. Dana, "are not ordinarily regarded as colors; but white and black objects are commonly spoken of as colored, although the former reflect and the latter absorb all the rays of light without separating them into colors properly so-called." What intervene between these two extremes are known as primary or simple colors, and mixed or complementary; and they are almost of infinite shades. That it is exceedingly difficult to speak with anything like

*Wm. C. Ward, Indep. July 28, '92.

precision where infinity prevails may be seen at once.
And this is precisely the condition of things that
meets us here. Nothing is more difficult to describe
as has been intimated above than the color of a person. The old Arabs as if they appreciated this fact,
to quote Dr. Prideaux Tregelles "distinguished but
two races, one red or ruddy which we call white, the
other black."†

Approaching as we do the color that was really in
the mind of Solomon, when he wrote:

"My beloved is white and ruddy."

we are led to ask, first: Can it be possible that he
used here a colloqualism? or a provincialism? Peoples of color, especially where the colors are varied,
have a peculiar way of referring to one another. Our
attention was first called to this by a good English friend.
"How strangely you use the word "bright." she said,
"in describing the colored people of the United States.
I have inquired the color of several, and you have said
to me, they were 'bright.' At first I was somewhat per
plexed to understand you. I perceive now that you
use that word to express the fact, that in complexion
they are quite light or fair, when compared to others."
We might be thought to draw largely on our imagi-
nation, if we were to argue the possibility of a similar

†אדם. p. xiii.

usus loquendi among the Hebrews of Solomon's day; nor will we. But supposing this to have been so, it would exactly suit the case, as we are sure it existed:

"My beloved is bright and ruddy;" that is, he is more fair than the average. How exactly that would suit the original, it is only necessary to consult the word employed. That the idea of comparison was in the mind of the bride who is made to speak, can. scarcely be doubted.

A moment before this Egyptian beauty had said:

> I am black and comely,

But,

> My beloved is white and ruddy.

A veritable comparison! Says James Freeman Clarke:* "This power of *comparison* gives definiteness and clearness to thought: we never can understand anything well but by comparing it to something else." It was clearly so with this bride. Compared to her own dusky complexion, Solomon was indeed bright, or even white, to which translation no serious objection could be made, were all things equal and normal; but they are not, and because they are not, let this Nehushtan,†—harmless indeed of itself, but destructive in its influence be ground to powder. And what has just been said in regard to comparison,

*"Self Culture," p. 134.
†2 Kings, 18: 4.

will be strengthened when the general antiphonal nature of this composition is called to mind; 1or is it not, as says David:

> "Deep calleth unto deep at the voice of thy waterspouts" (Psl. 42: 7).

But what has been the thought of the translators of the great Versions of this word? Let us aim to see. But let us first enquire as to the thought of the later generation of Hebrew scholars and writers? We are scarcely prepared to do this requiring as it would the critical study of what both the Talmuds and Targums say; and what the Rabbins in general have written. Therefore we relegate to the rising scholars of the race, to whom we have dedicated this little volume, this and all kindred subjects — at least for broad discusion. And yet there is this that we can say The Hebrew writers after Solomon, Biblical writers we mean, are the four Greater and the twelve Mincr prophets. It is not necessary that we name them. What was the thought of these as to the mat· ter discussed we have no possible way of knowing ; save as they themselves used the word that Solomon employed. This we have in a measure already done, and supposing them to have been as apt as he in the use of this mother tongue, it is safe to conclude that they did not understand him to say that he was of "white" blood.   Three of the four Greater prophets had occasion to use the word; but never in the sense of *white*, as has already been shown.   It is a little singular that not one of the twelve Minor prophets has occasion to use the word.

If we inquire concerning the writers of the Apocrypha, it is sufficient to say these chiefly employed the Greek and not the Hebrew tongue.   But let us come to the Versionists.   What thought the Greek translator, of this description of Solomon—those who translated the Septuagint?   We quote the Schaff-Herzog account of this Version of the Bible.   "The truth about its origin is, that Alexandria became, after the Dispersion, a centre of Jewish population and eventually of religion; but as time went on, the Jews, under Greek influence, lost command of Hebrew, and therefore required a translation of their sacred books in Greek.   The men who met this want differed very much in knowledge and skill, were of an indeterminate number, and of different periods, beginning with the time of Ptolemy Philadelphus (B. C. 280), and continuing until (B. C. 150).   The Pentateuch was first translated.   Previously there had been Targums; and it is likely, that, upon the margin of the Hebrew manuscripts, difficult words and sentences were translated, and that these were used in the final complete work. The translation of the rest of the canon was less necessary, and was more a piece of literary work. The translators were chiefly of Egyptian and particularly Alexandrian, birth and training, and therefore strongly Hellenistic."*

The translation these men give of the fifth chapter of Canticles and tenth verse—the word at least, which we read as "white," is, λευκός What is to be said of it, as bearing upon the question at issue?

We say, first: The Septuagint translation was made at a time when what is known as the Alexandrian age of Greek literature ruled, with Ptolemy Philadelphus as its head and inspiring genius, say, (B. C. 200-300). The writers contemporary or immediately following the translators, with their works, were Bion and his Idyllia, Theocritus and his, together with his *Syrinx*, Aratus and his *Phœnomena;* with such historians as Callimachus, and Polybius and Apollodorus; not to mention others. It is not to be supposed that all the writings of these have escaped the destruction consequent upon the passing of centuries, but a critical survey of the portion that did escape, with the manner in which they used the Greek,

---

*Schaff-Herzog, Cycl. Vol. Art. *Bible Versions.*

especially the word under consideration, would doubtless throw light upon our discussion. But the works of these as they are presented to the modern world are not at hand; and even though they were, the criticism that would be necessary to show to advantage the lights and shadows of the words employed, of necessity must be relegated to the rising scholarship of the race.

And yet there is this to be said that in the Greek, there are according to some authorities six words which signify white; other give but five. Of the five or six as the case may be, two may be said to be about equally clear cut in their signification: these are λευκος and Aργός The meaning, of the first of these as given is: *white, bright, clear, pure, transparent, serene* etc.; the meaning of the second, as given, is: *white, brilliant, resplendent,* etc. Were we to go no further, scarcely anything bearing upon the matter in hand could be reached. But, let us peer a little beyond the surface. These two words, whence came they?

We speak first of αργος. Of it the authorities substantially say: In Greek, Argos was *first,* the name of a dog:

"A dog was lying near,
And lifted up his head and pricked his ears.
'Twas Argus which the much enduring man
Ulysses long-before had reared."*

Second, a name given a number of Greek cities. *Third*, the name of a number of Greek characters. *Fourth*, there was Argus said to have had a·hundred eyes. *Fifth*, the same as αερχος, *idle, lazy, indolent* etc: *Sixth*, and last, the signification under consideration, *white, bright, resplendent* etc. The only thing of moment, here given, is the fact already stated that it is clear cut in its signification of *white or bright*. Fortunately, however, for our cause and for the truth itself, this was not the word the translators used.

Approaching the other word, λευχος, we are not certain but a glimmer of light, is given, it being the word used by the translators of the Septuagint. Indeed, we would feel the more sure of this, were we possessed of a full knowledge of the languages and literature cognate to that of the Old Testament, for it is in these that the word found its root. But we are not, and are therefore compelled to see even the Hebrew and Greek, through the light which Japhetic scholarship presents. What, we are persuaded a knowledge of the Arabic, Syriac and the dead lan-

---

*Bryant's Homer's Odyssey, Bk. XVII. 335-338.

guages of the East, in general, would give, is denied us; but we say, it will not be denied the goodly company of Afro-American scholars whose coming is already in view   It is said of Leverrier (Urbain Jean Joseph) that his studies in Astronomy convinced him that the movements of the planet Uranus "could not be explained by the attraction of any known bodies, and he accordingly sought further for the cause of its perturbations.   Finally, on June 1, 1846, he indicated to the Academy of sciences within 10° the place where a new planet might be seen on January 1, 1867   This was in fact done by the German astronomer Galle, who discovered it, however September 23, 1847   Leverrier had made an error, but only of 20° "*   And so we, presuming upon the trend of facts, similarly intimate that the coming scholarship of our variety of the common race, will find sufficient in relation to this Greek verb, as to show why it was preferred to all the others, in that it presented a phase of color other than that which Japheth means, especially the American branch of the family, when he speaks of a man being *white*   One reason for this, is found in the following fact as to the its derivation. We quote from   John Parkhurst;† who says substan-

*Art. Leverrier, Am. Cyc. Vol. p. 378.
†J. Parkhurst Lex. p. 412.

tially : This verb λευχός is from one which signifies *to see, look*, because things of a *white* color are *conspic-uous* or *easily seen*. And this last verb itself (the one which signifies *to see*) may be derived from another which signifies a *lion, on account of his sharp sight;* and this too is from a noun in Hebrew which also signifies a *lion*. Gesenius, however, says it was on account of his *strength* And we say on account of his *color* If not, why not? Brushing aside all the web that Japheth has unconsciously thrown around this and almost every great fact and character of the past, and coming directly to the fact, that the verb used by the men who translated Solomon's Hebrew into Greek, was a word that found its original root in a Hebrew word which signified a lion, in any discussion like to that which we are carrying on, it is altogether as reason-able to suppose that the color of the beast was as much a factor in giving significance to the word, as was his sharp sightedness or his strength. And again we ask : If not, why not? And the more especially when we remember that the color of the lion is given as the color of the people of the continent and local-ity in question, *to wit,* TAWNY or yellowish, the very word which many of the ethnologists employ But we may be told that such a surmise is foreign to the use of the word.

5

Possibly so, as it pertains to the Japhetic use of it. But how about its use by peoples kindred to those who first developed it from its Hebrew original? We cannot doubt as heretofore intimated that the color of the beast, was quite as likely to come in for consideration, as was his sagacity or his strength. And we may well believe was so understood by the ancient scholars of the Orient, the very men who made the translation in question: for they were "Egyptians and particularly of Alexandrian birth," with whom color was altogether as potential in the conception of facts, as aught else. At least, Japheth says they were Egyptians. Shem however declares them to have been Hebrews; six out of each the Twelve Tribes * Exactly why the testimony of Josephus should be so unceremoniously brushed aside is certainly not clear. He is exceedingly minute, to be sure; but no more so, than in all else he writes. In either case they were men of the East, and were utterly free from all that characterizes the white races of the West, especially those of these last days who have unconsciously warped every great fact of the past; Christianity itself not excepted. A brief illustration of this last remark, is the word of a commentator†

*Josephus Ant. XII : II : 1.
†Phila. Ledger, Mar. 16, '95.

on the words of Christ: "Zaccheus, make haste! I must abide at thy house." Says this commentator: "In this country such a salutation would be an act of great rudeness. Not so among Orientalists. They held hospitality as an exalted privilege and virtue (Gen. 18: 3-5). It was even enjoined upon Christians (Heb. 13: 2)." According to this critic, the peoples of Europe and America, presume to say not only what is good manners, even in the Christ; but what is good morals; for if Christianity enjoin such hospitality as the Orientalists practiced, why do not the Christians of the West, practice it? Are they not Christian? Do they propose to stand by the condition? "Ye are my friends, if ye do the things I command you" (John 15: 14)? The one reason and only reason, why this is not done, is. that Japheth colors everything to suit himself.

As we see it, the "white," of Canticles as seen by these Alexandrian translators is the brightness, say, of the lion clean and fresh and beautiful from his lair, when tinged with the rays of the sun. And of this, we are all the more sure, when we call to mind the signification they give the word, which we have as "ruddy" It is nothing less than a Greek word ($\pi\nu\rho\rho\sigma$) which signifies, *red, of a fiery color; flame-colored,* as some lexicographers put it. Taking, then, the testi-

mony of this Greek Version as we find it in the
Septuagint, we could not possibly wish for one more
in harmony with our thought of the Hebrew and
therefore more conclusive of our position.

By common consent the next great Version after the
Septuagint is, that that is known as the Vulgate.
We give our readers what Thomas Hartwell Horne*
says: "This version, which surpasses all former ones,
was executed at different times, Jerome having translated particular books in the order requested by his
friends. We learn from Augustine that it was introduced into the churches by degrees, for fear of offend-
ing weak persons: at length it acquired so great an
authority from the approbation it received from Pope
Gregory I., that ever since the seventh century it has
been exclusively adopted by the Roman Catholic
church, under the name of the Vulgate version: and
a decree of the Council of Trent, in the sixteenth century, commanded that the Vulgate alone should be
used whenever the Bible is publicly read, and in all
sermons, expositions and disputations; and pronounced
it to be AUTHENTIC,—a very ambiguous term, which
ought to have been more precisely defined, than the
members of that council chose to define it."

In the strongest possible sense, this version is thor-

*Horne On the Scriptures. Vol. II. p. 198.

oughly Japhetic; or to the extent that is possible with the word of God. Such a remark as this, is based on the translation of a single word, and that a small one, the word for which the sixth letter in the Hebrew alphabet stands. "This particle(ו) is very widely extended in its use, since the Hebrews, in many cases in which sentences require to be connected, did not make any precise distinction of the manner of the connection; and thus in the simplicity of an ancient language, they made use of this one copula, in cases in which, in more cultivated languages, adversative, causal or final particles would be used. To its use is to be ascribed, very often, a certain looseness of expression in Hebrew "* In the face of this use of this particle; as well as the fact that the adversative nature of the clause is largely to him who will have it so, there is no possible apology for Jerome changing what Solomon wrote and what the Greek translators of the Septuagint recognized. Solomon had his bride to say :

"I am black and comely,

The Greeks recognized the force of this, *and*, and kept it in the text. Jerome, however, saw an adversative in it and so translated it:

"I am black but comely"

*Ges. Lex. V p. 233.

From him all others of his race have taken their cue;
and the idea remains of a black queen in an age when
black was popular and was in authority, apologizing
for her blackness!

From such a temper as this, we have little to hope
according to our way of thinking, as to the significance of the words:

"My beloved is white and ruddy,"

And yet even Jerome was so inspired with the thought
that other than white, pure and simple, was intended,
that he used neither *albus* nor *albens*, but *candidus*.
The first two of these words, in their *primary* signification, mean *white*, as even a slight reference to Latin
literature will show Not so with the word Jerome
saw fit to employ, *candidus*, whose primary signification, is in perfect harmony with the Hebrew original,
bright, orient, shining.

We have seemed to emphasize just here, the fact of
the primary signification of these words. Nor is this
unimportant. On the contrary, the primary signification of a word may be said to be the atmosphere
through which the word, ever after should be seen.
Usage may in time seem to nullify its significance;
but unconsciously it holds sway, and any interpreta-

tion of the writing of those who lived in what may be
called the days of its origin, that does not take it into account, is wrong to the extent this is done. Jerome
could have used *albus* or *albens*, whose more than primary signification is white; but he did not; choosing
rather a word that in all strictness may be said to
mean white incidentally and not necessarily—for there
is such a thing as bright or shining black. *Candidus*,
is really expressive of no color in particular, but the
brightness of any. And in this, it is at one, with the
Hebrew, *Stach*. Nor can one forego just here, express-
ing the regret that he had not proved as faithful in
the case of the queen; and that the mortal fear of
changing the Septuagint which he is said to have en-
tertained had prevented him here as elsewhere. Then
indeed would woes not a few have been saved a hap-
less race; for it cannot be denied that mountains of
our grief are to be laid at the door of the theologians.

Jerome, however, lived and wrote in what is known
as the brazen age of Roman literature, comprised,
say, in the interval from A. D. 118 to A. D. 410, or
from the death of Trajan to the coming of the Gauls.
Dr. Andrews gives the names of thirty five writers
of this age. How *candidus* was used by these, were
it possible to have them before us, would doubtless
demonstrate what is readily seen in anything like a

close perusal of the Vulgate, *to wit*, for a thing unquestionably white, the word chiefly used is *albus;*
and that *candidus*, embraces primarily the *shining* or
bright element. But the full verification of this, also,
in so far as its accomplishment is possible, we turn
over to our younger and more broadly equipped
scholars.

Our last word, in relation to the testimony of the
Vulgate, refers to the word, *ruddy*. Its word, is not,
rubicundulus, *somewhat red, or ruddy;* but, rubicun-
dus, *ruddy, blood-red, very red.*

These are the standard versions of Christendom.
All others, German, French, English are but second-
ary, taking as their cue, what these two say—possibly excepting the English which is made directly from
the Hebrew. Could we be sure of the interpretation
of the Commentators, we should be quite willing to
rest our case.

INTERPRETATIVE HELPS OR PROOFS.

We approach the last section of our Monograph. We have aimed to analyze critically the words the wise son of David had his Egyptian bride to use. In addition we have given the testimony of Ethnology and of the great Versions, as these were supposed to bear upon the matter discussed. Lastly we give what some, not all, for their name is legion, of the leading interpretators of the Bible, English, of course, have to say We deem it well to give in connection with what they say, a very brief word, as to who they are; for nothing so greatly helps in correctly estimating words or opinions as a knowledge however brief, of who the speaker is. We cannot do better than give first the comment of the Targum* or Chaldean Para

---

* "The word, *Targum*, signifies an exposition, or interpretation or a translation of one language into another; and here of the Hebrew text into the Chaldee language, with an explanation. The first use of these translations was after the return of the Jews from Babylon, where they had almost lost the Hebrew language; and, therefore, was necessary for the understanding of the law and the prophets. The translation of the five books of Moses was done by Onkelos and that of the prophets by Jonathan Ben Uzziel, the former of whom lived a little after Christ, and the latter a little before him: but the translation of the Hagiographa among which is this book of Canticles, is generally thought to have been done by R. Joseph Cæcus. The paraphrase on this book could not have been till after the finishing of the Talmud, seeing express mention is made of it there.

phrase, supposedly made by Rabbi Joseph Cæcus.
The paraphrase on the Song of Songs, says Dr. Adam
Clarke, "could not have been written till after the
Talmud, seeing express mention is made of it there.
The words of the Rabbi Canticles 5: 10 are: "Wherefore the congregation of Israel began to speak in
praise of the Lord of the world, and thus she said,
That God I desire to serve who in the day is covered
with a garment white as snow, and the brightness
of the glory of the Lord, whose face shines as fire"
etc.   We give next the comment of

REV A. R. FAUSSET, A.M.

Excepting the fact that he hailed from St. Cuth-
bert's York, England, it has been next to impossible
to find aught concerning this most scholarly divine;
save that in conjunction with Rev Dr. Robert Jam-
ieson of St. Paul's Glasgow, Scotland and the Rev
Dr. David Brown, Professor of Theology, Aberdeen
Scotland, he gave the Church a Critical and Explana-
tory Commentary on the Bible—and this, despite the
fact that we ran through ten or more Biographical
Cyclopædias on our shelf.   But let his words declare
him, for, notwithstanding the fact, he spiritualizes
the entire Song, yet what he says, is singularly
apropos the subject discussed.   In his Comment on
Canticles (5: 10), he says:

"The Hebrew for *white*, is properly, *illuminated by the sun*, ' white as the light ' (Matt. 17: 2); *red*, in His blood dyed garments as slain (Isaiah 63: 1-3. Revelation 5:6. 19: 13)."

JOHN GILL,

a learned Bible expositor of the Baptist faith. He was born Nov 23, 1697 at Kettering England. His school education, we are told was limited; but by hard sturdy he attained to eminence as a scholar, especially as an Orientalist. He is said to have learned Hebrew without any assistance. So passionately fond was he of books, that it became a proverb: "As sure as that John Gill is in the bookseller's shop." Singularly enough, his first effort as a commentator was on Solomon's Song: and Mr. Spurgeon pronounces the effort, as "invaluable in its own line of things." He died at Camberwell, October 14, 1771. It will be observed that he allegorized the Canticles. Upon the verse under consideration, he says: "Some understand this of the two natures in Christ, divine and human; with respect to his divine nature, *white*, expressive of his simplicity, purity and holiness: * * * * * with respect to his human, *red*, being a partaker of the same flesh and blood with his people. * * * * But it may denote in general, his fair

ness, beauty and glory; being as a divine person, the
brightness of his Father's glory; as man fairer than
the children of men."

THOMAS SCOTT

was born at Braytoft, England, February 16, 1747
and died at Aston, Sandford, April 16, 1821. To not
a few of our struggling ministry, the following may
be read with profit: "At the age of sixteen he was
bound apprentice to a medical practitioner at Alford,
but at the end of his months the master was dissatis-
fied with his behavior, and sent him home He was
now employed about the farm for some time, and
compelled to labor in the most menial occupations—
sometimes tending the sheep, and at others following
the plough. In this menial situation he continued for
more than nine years, yet continually cherishing the
wish to become a clergyman." By upright living and
hard study his wish was finally obtained; and by
continued study he has enrolled his name among those
of the great scholars of the Church.

What he says of Canticles 5: 10, is very brief: "In
this description some reference is supposed to be had
by the sacred writer to his father David, who was
'ruddy and of a fair countenance,' and who was celebrated as having slain his ten thousand; for the

words 'chief among' may signify lifting up a standard over ten thousand."

DR. SYMON PATRICK.

He was Lord Bishop of Ely, England. He was born 1626 at Gamsborough in Lincolnshire, and died at his See, May 31, 1707 He was educated at Queen's College, Cambridge, where he became a fellow in 1648.* His words on the verse discussed, are, having the bride speak:

"My beloved * * * is of princely form, having admirable beauty and sweetness, mixed with equal majesty and brightness * * * * And whether we translate the first words, 'white and ruddy,' as in our Bible; or as Bochart 'white and shining or glistening,' it matters not. For it only signifies in my opinion, the majestic beauty of his aspect."

MATTHEW HENRY

was an eminent Non Conformist minister. His father was Philip Henry, one of the two thousand who left the Church of England rather than conform to the "Act of Uniformity " Matthew was born in Flintshire, Wales, Oct. 28, 1662. He was educated at Islington. He first thought of the Law as a profession and early entered Gray's Inn. But his call to the

---

*See Schaff-Herzog, Vol. III. p. 1765.

ministry was too apparent both to him and his friends.
For twenty five years he ministered to a church at
Chester. In 1712, he was called to Hackney, London.
It is said of him: "At the commencement of his
ministry, he began with the first chapter of Genesis
in the forenoon, and the first chapter of Matthew in
the afternoon." He died June 22, 1714. Speaking
to a friend, he said: "You have been used to take
notice of the sayings of dying men; this is mine:
that a life spent in the service of God and communion
with him, is the most pleasant life that any one can
live in this world." The comment of this scholarly
divine is altogether spiritual and is as follows:

" His love to us renders him lovely   He is *white* in
the spotless innocency of his life, *ruddy* in the bloody
sufferings he went through at his death; *white* in his
glory, as God; *ruddy* in his assuming the nature of
man, *Adam—red earth; white* in his tenderness toward
his people, *ruddy* in his terrible appearances against
his and their enemies."

There is scarcely a name better known in the English speaking world, than

ADAM CLARKE

a Wesleyan Methodist minister and distinguished as
a divine, an antiquarian and an Oriental scholar.
When he was born is not definitely known, for his

mother, like the mother of Douglass and many of our people, could not fix the day It has generally been put down at 1760 or 1762, and at Moybeg, London-derry, Co., Ireland. He was of the class known as Scotch Irish. He was licensed to preach in his twen-tieth year; or in the year 1778, at least, he joined conference. His immense attainments as a scholar are chiefly to be credited to his industry, for as is well known when young he seemed rather stupid. He died at Bayswater Middlesex England, August 26, 1832. Dr. Clarke utterly repudiated the idea of Canticles being a spiritual allegory, representing the love of Christ and his church. He says: "It is much better, therefore, if explained or illustrated at all, to take it in its literal meaning, and explain it in its general sense." What he here says, he did; therefore his comment on chapter five, verse tenth is exceedingly brief: "*Red* and *white*, properly mixed, are essential to a fine complexion; and this is what is intimated: he has the finest complexion among ten thousand persons."

JOHANN PETER LANGE —PHILIP SCHAFF.

Lange, the first mentioned of these two great schol-ars of the church, was born in Sournborn, near Elber-field, Germany, April 10, 1802. He was a student at

Bonn. In the thirty-ninth year of his age he re
ceived a call as professor of theology to the Zurich.
While here he wrote his great work: *Life of Jesus.*
In 1854, he was called to Bonn.   While here he wrote
the work by which he is best known, his *Theological and
Homiletical Bible Work.*   It is from the English trans·
lation of this great commentary, made by Dr. Schaff
in conjunction with many scholars, that we quote.

Dr. Schaff next mentioned was born at Coire,
Switzerland, January 1, 1819.   In a sense he was the
product of all the great universities of Germany,
having studied at Stuttgart in the gymnasium; and
then at Tubingen, Halle and Berlin, at which last
place he lectured on exegesis and church history.
Upon the recommendation of such men as Neander,
Tholuck and Julius Muller, he was called to a pro-
fessorship at Mercersburg, Penn., in 1,843, and filled
it for twenty years, or until 1863.   He has recently
died.   As a scholar and Biblicist, he can scarcely be
said to have an equal.

In the translation he has given of Lange's Comment
on Canticles 5: 10, we find the following:

"'My beloved is white and ruddy, distinguished
above ten thousand.''   This general statement pre·
cedes the more detailed description of the beauties of

her lover, when there follows vers. 11–15 in ten par
ticulars, at the close of which (ver. 16) stands another
general eulogium.   The aim of the entire description
is evidently to depict Solomon, as one who is without
blemish from head to foot, as is done 2 Sam. XIV 25,
26, in the case of his brother Absalom.   A commen-
dation of his fair color, or his good looks in general
fitly stands at the head of the description.   His face
might very well be called ruddy or brownish (as 1
Sam. XVI. 12) but scarcely dazzling white; and it is
to the face that the predicate mainly refers, as a comparison with vers. 14 and 15 shows.''

5

SECTION VI.

RESUME.

We cannot better finish our Monograph than by a Resume.

Ethnography showed that as Europe had a people peculiar in color and hair texture; and Africa the same, even so with Asia. In common parlance the European is white, with straight hair; the Asiatic yellow with curly hair; the African black with crisped hair. On general principles, therefore, Solomon being an Asiatic would be of a yellow complexion and black curly hair. Nor will the fact of the border location of his realm in the least affect what might be taken for granted. On the contrary, the most likely effect such position would have, would be to increase the color of his face and make more crispy the curliness of his hair; for all his contact was with the darker tribes and nations of the South and Southwest. To suppose any change of color and hair from contact with the tribes and peoples of the North and North-west, is scarcely supposable. As a matter of fact Solomon was doubtless a fine specimen of the southwest Semitic race, whose bright golden color and whose raven locks were the pride of the daughter of Pasebchanu II, the reigning Pharaoh of Egypt, if we are to believe what Wendel (F. C. H) says.*

The one proof the section on Linguistics gave, supports what has been said above: in this that it de clares the king to be ruddy or red.   Primarily our discussion centres on the word, "white" and not on ruddy   Any wide awake reader will doubtless have discovered that the word there translated "white," largely expends its strength not in telling us the color of the king, *but the condition of that color.*   Whatever his color was, that word simply and only tells us that it was bright or shining. Supposing him to have been black, that word, largely adjectival in its signification, would tell us that he was a bright or shining black. Supposing him to have been yellow, it tells us he was a bright yellow; and the same is true, supposing him to have been white. As we are sure he was not black, we are equally sure he was not white. What his color was, was ruddy; and his rud-diness was bright. Bright, then, is the word, and not white. That this is the case, the reader has only

*Hist. of Egypt. F. C. H. Wendel, p. 108.

to refer to the section on Linguistics. As is there shown, the idea of bright, is the one idea that is manifest in every phase of the word. As is said: "* * the signification of shining and being bright is widely extended in the roots from the biliteral stock * * also in those beginning with the softened letters * * and without any sibilant." The condition of the color, we say, and not the color itself, is what the word signifies—such a condition as is seen when the sun shines upon an object.

Essentially the proofs of the Versional section are the same; at least we think so. Nor are we at all inclined to shrink from the manifest difficulty and un certainty of these proofs. As to what the Septuagint says, we feel to reiterate the legitimacy of the argument made, for the color of the lion—whence the root is found, for his color was as likely to impress, especially in the glare of the sun, as any other of the leonine qualities. As to the Vulgate, it is altogether as much to the point, as any could expect. Jerome's choice of the word *candidus*, instead of *candidulus*, is significant of the deepness of the color, with which the Hebrew original had impressed him. But like our own Bible, both Authorized and Revised, these are but human translations and lay no claim to the inspiration of the Original. And it is to this Original all must defer, whether Greek or Latin, King James or Douay

The proofs of the Interpretative section. speak for themselves. While indeed but few of them take the trouble to show the real trend of the word employed, satisfying themselves with the word "white," yet with only an exception here and there, the idea of *brightness* always comes in for notice. Nor is it necessary for us to restate what they say; but only invite the reader to return and ponder upon the significant fact. It is to be said, however, of the very few who considered technically the word, that they are singularly just and outspoken. This is especially true of Fausset (A. R.) who frankly admits that the Hebrew for *white*, is properly, *illuminated by the sun;* and what is that but saying he was bright. Nor is Schaff any the less clear spoken. His words are: "His face might very well be called ruddy or brownish, but scarcely daz zlingly white "

The only conclusion that possibly can be reached is that the word, " white," as used in our translation — by the good queen :

"My beloved is white and ruddy"

should really be translated—and we say it with all

possible respect for the scholarship of the men who made it:

"My beloved is bright and ruddy."

This whole discussion may seem to be "only an eager bustling, that rather keeps ado, than does any-thing."[*] But we do not so deem it and beg to refer the reader to our words Preliminary to the work proper. In times like these when we read constantly of the "White City," the "White Squadron," the "White Race" etc etc., it is in place to show that there is something worthy of consideration, that can not be made to sail under this banner. To this end, do we write. And to this end, do we commit this subject to the rising scholars of our "race."

*Earle's Microcosm 27: 58.

INDEX OF AUTHORS AND SUBJECTS.

www.ingramcontent.com/pod-product-compliance
Lightning Source LLC
Chambersburg PA
CBHW020034030726
47499CB00007B/2420